Dear Parents and Educators,

Welcome to Penguin Young Readers! As parents and educators, you know that each child develops at his or her own pace—in terms of speech, critical thinking, and, of course, reading. Penguin Young Readers recognizes this fact. As a result, each Penguin Young Readers book is assigned a traditional easy-to-read level (1–4) as well as a Guided Reading Level (A–P). Both of these systems will help you choose the right book for your child. Please refer to the back of each book for specific leveling information. Penguin Young Readers features esteemed authors and illustrators, stories about favorite characters, fascinating nonfiction, and more!

Bones and the Big Yellow Mystery

LEVEL **3**

GUIDED READING LEVEL **K**

This book is perfect for a **Transitional Reader** who:
- can read multisyllable and compound words;
- can read words with prefixes and suffixes;
- is able to identify story elements (beginning, middle, end, plot, setting, characters, problem, solution); and
- can understand different points of view.

Here are some **activities** you can do during and after reading this book:
- Summarize: Using his detective skills, Jeffrey Bones is able to solve the big yellow mystery. Once you've finished reading the book, use your memory to summarize what happened to Mr. Green's bus.
- Character Traits: Bones is the main character in this story. Come up with a list of words to describe him.

Remember, sharing the love of reading with a child is the best gift you can give!

—Bonnie Bader, EdM
  Penguin Young Readers program

*Penguin Young Readers are leveled by independent reviewers applying the standards developed by Irene Fountas and Gay Su Pinnell in *Matching Books to Readers: Using Leveled Books in Guided Reading*, Heinemann, 1999.

For my great-niece, Maayan Malca—DA

For my son, David: Your astounding
talents inspire me—BJN

Penguin Young Readers
Published by the Penguin Group
Penguin Group (USA) Inc., 375 Hudson Street, New York, New York 10014, USA
Penguin Group (Canada), 90 Eglinton Avenue East, Suite 700, Toronto, Ontario M4P 2Y3, Canada
(a division of Pearson Penguin Canada Inc.)
Penguin Books Ltd., 80 Strand, London WC2R 0RL, England
Penguin Group Ireland, 25 St. Stephen's Green, Dublin 2, Ireland (a division of Penguin Books Ltd.)
Penguin Group (Australia), 250 Camberwell Road, Camberwell, Victoria 3124, Australia
(a division of Pearson Australia Group Pty. Ltd.)
Penguin Books India Pvt. Ltd., 11 Community Centre, Panchsheel Park, New Delhi—110 017, India
Penguin Group (NZ), 67 Apollo Drive, Rosedale, Auckland 0632, New Zealand
(a division of Pearson New Zealand Ltd.)
Penguin Books (South Africa) (Pty.) Ltd., 24 Sturdee Avenue,
Rosebank, Johannesburg 2196, South Africa

Penguin Books Ltd., Registered Offices: 80 Strand, London WC2R 0RL, England

Text copyright © 2004 by David A. Adler. Illustrations copyright © 2004 by Barbara Johansen Newman.
All rights reserved. First published in 2004 by Viking and in 2008 by Puffin Books, imprints of
Penguin Group (USA) Inc. Published in 2012 by Penguin Young Readers, an imprint of
Penguin Group (USA) Inc., 345 Hudson Street, New York, New York 10014. Manufactured in China.

The Library of Congress has cataloged the Viking edition
under the following Control Number: 2004000824

ISBN 978-0-14-241042-4   10 9 8 7 6 5 4 3 2 1

BONES
and the Big Yellow Mystery

For Joseph,

David A Adler

by David A. Adler
illustrated by Barbara Johansen Newman

Penguin Young Readers
An Imprint of Penguin Group (USA) Inc.

Contents

Chapter 1
My Name Is Bones

My name is Bones.

Jeffrey Bones.

I find clues.

I solve mysteries.

One afternoon I took my detective

bag and went with Grandpa

to the shopping mall.

It's a big place with lots of people

and lots of clues.

We went to the corner store.

I took detective powder

from my detective bag

and sprinkled some on the door.

"Hey, look," I said.

"Fingerprints! Lots of fingerprints!"

"Don't look for clues," Grandpa told me.

"Look for shirts."

"I can do that," I said.

I can read now,

so it's easy for me to find things.

I read the signs.

Signs are clues.

"Follow me," I said,

and Grandpa did.

"Look," I said.

"Lots of shirts!"

"I only need one," Grandpa told me.

I found him the best one.

It had stripes and pockets.

My name is Bones,

Jeffrey Bones.

I find clues.

I find shirts.

"Let's not go home," I said.

"Let's go to the pet shop."

I read the signs and found it.

In the window

was a puppy with curly hair.

"Hello, Curly," I said.

Curly wagged his curly tail.

I took my bad-man disguise

from my detective bag.

I put it on and walked back and forth.

Curly followed me.

I took off my disguise.

"He's a good detective dog," I said.

"He knows how to follow bad men."

"He likes you," Grandpa said.

"I like him, too," I said.

"I want a dog," I told Grandpa,

"but Mom and Dad said I'm too young."

Grandpa nodded.

"Hey, Jeffrey," someone said.

I turned.

It was Mr. Green, my school bus driver.

"Look at Detective Dog Curly," I said.

Mr. Green looked at Curly,

and I looked at Mr. Green.

He looked worried.

Mr. Green said, "I need you."

"Sure you do," I told him.

"Everyone needs Bones."

Chapter 2
I Was Right

Grandpa laughed and said,

"Of course everyone needs bones.

We need bones to stand and walk."

"This is serious," Mr. Green said.

"I lost my bus.

I need Jeffrey to find it."

I took out my pad.

"The big yellow one with wheels?"

I asked.

"Yes," Mr. Green said.

I wrote *Big*, *Yellow*, and *Wheels*

on my pad.

"A bus is a big thing to lose,"

I told Mr. Green.

"But don't worry.

I find things.

I'll find your bus."

"Maybe someone stole it,"

Mr. Green said.

"Maybe someone did," I told him.

"And maybe not."

I showed him my pad.

"I already have three clues:

Big, Yellow, and *Wheels.*"

I asked Mr. Green to show us

where he left his bus.

"Sure," he said.

"Come with me."

I took out my magnifying glass.

It makes little things big.

It helps me find clues, even little clues.

We followed Mr. Green to the parking lot.

"I left it right there," he said.

He pointed to a row of cars.

"It took up four spots."

I looked through my

magnifying glass.

I didn't see a bus.

But I did see lots of cars.

"These cars are so big," I said.

"Put away your glass," Grandpa said.

"Oh."

Without my glass,

the cars were not so big.

"Hey," I said, and pointed.

"That's Grandpa's car."

And I was right.

"But what about my bus?"

Mr. Green asked.

"It's not here," I said.

I was right about that, too.

Chapter 3
Green for Mr. Green

"What did you do,"

I asked Mr. Green,

"after you parked your bus?"

He pointed to the corner store.

"I went in there," he said,

"and bought this shirt."

It was a green striped shirt.

"Green for Mr. Green," Grandpa said.

He laughed.

I didn't.

Green Shirt,

I wrote on my pad.

I had lots of clues

but no big yellow bus.

"Show us where

you bought the shirt," I said.

We followed Mr. Green.

We walked into the store,

and Mr. Green said,

"The men's shirts are just past

the suits, coats, and shoes."

"No," I said.

"Look at the sign.

Signs are clues.

The shirts are right here."

"Oh yes," Mr. Green said.

"After I bought this shirt,

I went to the parking lot,

and my bus was gone."

I looked at Mr. Green.

He looked at me.

"Well," he asked,

"can you help me find my bus?"

Well, I thought.

I found shirts.

I found the pet shop and Curly.

Will I find Mr. Green's big yellow bus?

Chapter 4
I Needed to Think

I needed to know more.

"You couldn't find your bus," I said,

"so you looked for me?"

"No," Mr. Green told me.

"I looked for a telephone.

I called my boss and told him

I had lost my bus."

We followed Mr. Green to the telephones.

"I walked here and saw you," he said.

We were near the pet shop.

Curly saw me and wagged his curly tail.

I looked at my pad.

I looked at the clues.

Big, Yellow, Wheels, and *Green Shirt.*

I thought about the missing bus.

I walked back and forth.

Sometimes that helps me think.

Curly walked back and forth, too.

Curly was thinking, too.

I walked to the telephones.

Curly left the pet shop window.

The pet shop door was open.

Curly walked out.

"Hey," I said.

"What are you doing here?"

Curly wagged his curly tail.

"Hey," I said.

"Go back to the pet shop."

Curly barked and wagged his curly tail.

"Go back," I told Curly.

"Go back the way you came."

Grandpa took Curly back

the way he came.

"What about my bus?" Mr. Green asked.

I thought about Mr. Green

and I thought about Curly.

Just then, I did it!

I solved the mystery

of the big yellow bus.

Chapter 5
Let's Go Back

I smiled and told Mr. Green,

"Go back the way you came."

Mr. Green said,

"But that's what you told Curly."

"And that's what you should do," I said.

Mr. Green didn't understand.

"Follow me," I said.

Mr. Green followed me

into the corner store.

"You bought a shirt here," I said.

"Then you went out that door

to the parking lot."

"Yes," Mr. Green said.

"And my bus was gone."

"But you didn't come in

through that door," I told him.

"You came in over there."

I pointed to a different door.

"When you came in you walked past

the suits, coats, and shoes.

Now let's go back
the way you came."
Mr. Green followed me
past the suits, coats, and shoes and
through the door.
We walked outside,
and there, in four parking spots,
was his big yellow bus.

"Thank you.

Thank you," Mr. Green said.

"You found my lost bus."

"Your bus wasn't lost," I told him.

"It was here all the time."

Mr. Green smiled and said,

"Let's go back to your grandfather."

"Not yet," I said.

"First I must check my clues."

I looked at the bus.

It was big.

It was yellow.

It had wheels.

I checked those clues.

"Where's your shirt?" I asked.

Mr. Green showed it to me.

It was green, so I checked that, too.

I put my detective pad in my
detective bag with all my
detective things.

"Now we can go," I said.

"I have solved the mystery
of the big yellow bus."

Mr. Green took me to Grandpa.
Grandpa was outside the pet shop
with bags of dog food—and Curly.
"Curly is coming home with me,"
Grandpa said.

"I'm not too young to have a dog.

I'm not too young for anything."

Curly wagged his curly tail.

He licked my face.

"I found lots of things today," I said.

"I found clues, shirts,

and a big yellow bus.

But best of all,

I found Detective Dog Curly."

Curly wagged his curly tail

and licked my face.

"Curly likes Bones," I said.

Grandpa laughed and said,

"All dogs like bones.

They chew on them."

"Well," I said,

"Curly likes this Bones.

Detective Jeffrey Bones.

Curly likes me."